Good Night, I Love You

Caroline Jayne Church

Hodder Children's Books

It's time for bed,
so let's get ready.

Bring your bunny,
bring your teddy.

Bath fun at the
end of the day!

Laugh, splash,
giggle and play!

Scrub high,
scrub low.

Squeaky clean
from head to toe.

Wrapped up in towels,
lovely and dry.

Time to brush,
now open wide!

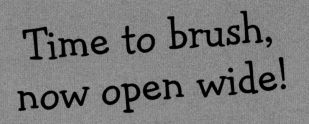

Toothbrushes up,

get dressed,
sleepyhead.

A night-time story,

let's read before bed.

Snuggle the covers

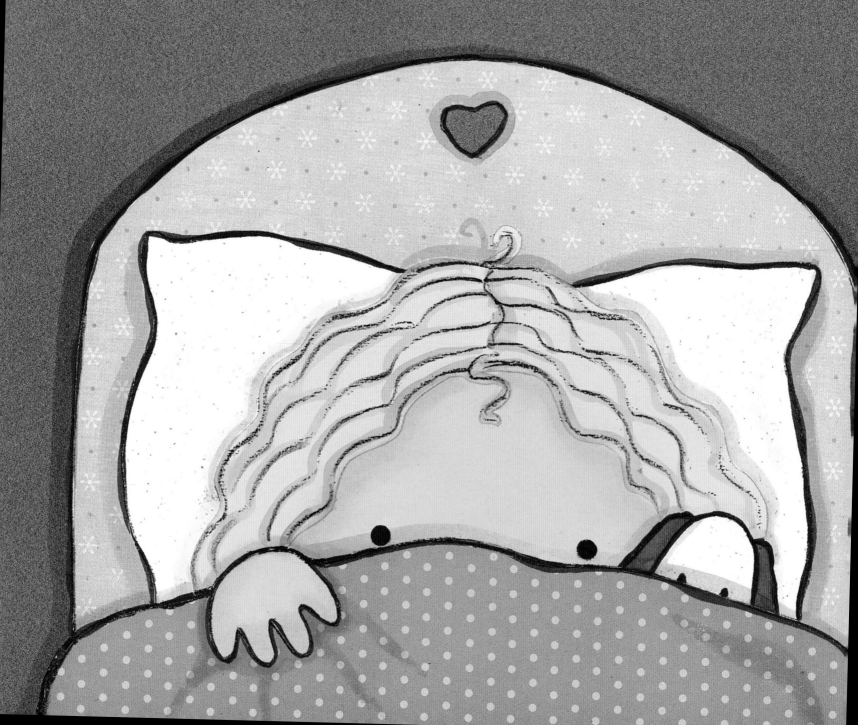

and off with the light.

Dream little dreams,

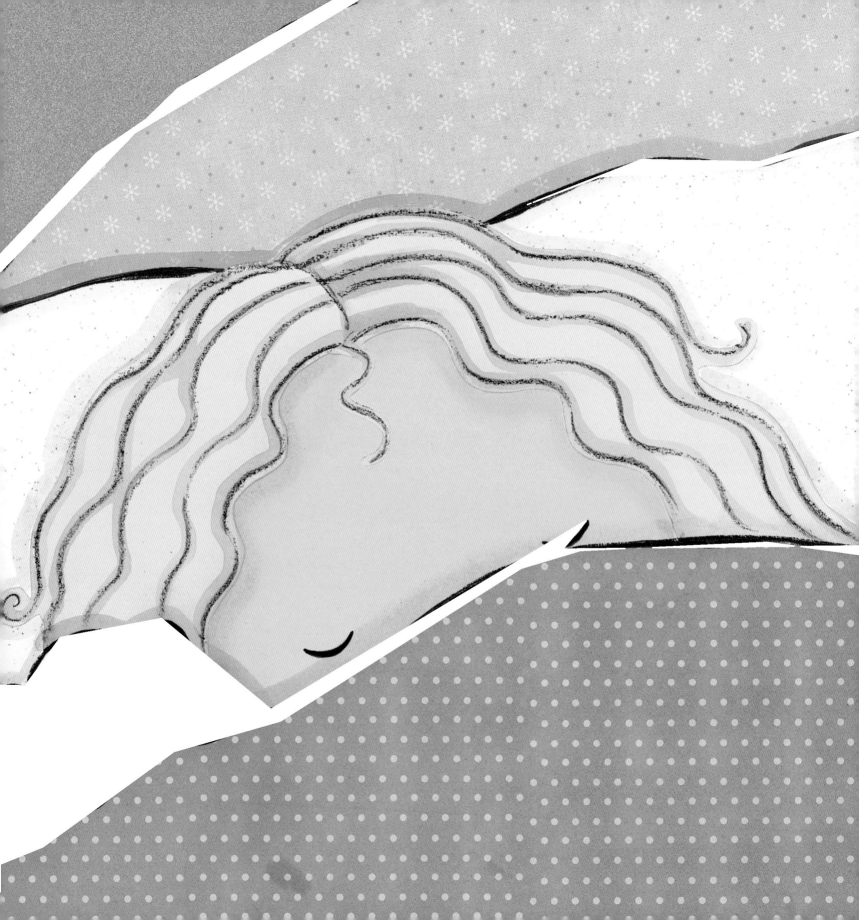

I love you,
good night.

For little Fred,
– CJC

First published in 2012 by Scholastic Inc.
This edition published in 2016 by Hodder Children's Books

Text and illustrations copyright © Caroline Jayne Church 2012

Hodder Children's Books
An imprint of Hachette Children's Group
Part of Hodder & Stoughton
Carmelite House
50 Victoria Embankment
London EC4Y 0DZ

Hachette Ireland
8 Castlecourt
Castleknock
Dublin 15, Ireland

A catalogue record of this book is available from the British Library.

ISBN: 978 1 444 96214 7

10 9 8 7 6 5 4 3 2 1

Printed in China

An Hachette UK Company
www.hachette.co.uk

MIX
Paper from
responsible sources
FSC® C104740